10th ANNIVERSARY EDITION

LIBRARY OF DOOM

THE BOOK THAT DRIPPED BLOOD

by Michael Dahl

Illustrated by Bradford Kendall

Library of Doom is published by Stone Arch Books,
A Capstone Imprint
1710 Roe Crest Drive
North Mankato, Minnesota 56003
www.mycapstone.com

Library of Congress Cataloging-in-Publication
Data is available on the Library of
Congress website.

ISBN: 978-1-4965-5529-8 (library binding)
ISBN: 978-1-4965-5535-9 (paperback)
ISBN: 978-1-4965-5541-0 (eBook PDF)

Summary: Can the Librarian stop a sharp-toothed
book from attacking innocent people?

Designer: Brent Slingsby

Photo credits:
Design Element: Shutterstock: Shebeko.

Printed and bound in the USA.
112017   010943R

Table of Contents

Ink from its pages oozes out
and covers the floor.

The puddle of ink grows larger.

A tall, dark shape rises . . .

THE LIBRARIAN

Real name: unknown
Parents: unknown
Birthplace/birthdate: unknown
Weaknesses: water, crumbs, dirty fingers
Strengths: speed reading, ability to fly

THE LIBRARY

The Library of Doom is the world's largest collection of strange and dangerous books. Each generation, a new Librarian is chosen to serve as guardian. The Librarian's duty is to keep the books from falling into the hands of those who would use them for evil.

The location of the Library of Doom is unknown. Its shelves sit partially hidden underground. Some sections form a maze. It is full of black holes. This means someone might walk down a hallway in the Library and not realize they are traveling thousands of miles. One hallway could start somewhere under the Atlantic Ocean and end inside the caves of the Himalayas.

There are entries to the Library scattered all over the earth. But there are few exits. Sometimes villains find their way into the vast collection, but the Librarian always finds them out!

— From *The Atlas Cryptical*, compiled by Orson Drood, 5th official Librarian

CHAPTER ONE

THE GOLDEN HINGES

A young man hurries down a dark street. Cuts and bruises cover his face. His left arm is in a sling.

In his right hand, he carries a package tied with thick rope.

At the end of the street, he finds what he is looking for. He walks into a **small bookstore**.

An older man, bent and wrinkled, stands behind a counter.

"Do you buy used books?" asks the young man.

"What do you have?" asks the old man.

The young man throws his package down on the counter.

The old storekeeper unties the thick rope and opens the package.

"Is this made of fur?" asks the old man.

"Look at the spine," says the younger man.

The old man turns the book on its side.

Two yellow hinges hold the book together.

"They're made of gold," says the young man. "How much will you give me for it?"

The old man pulls out a handful of cash and hands it to the young man. The young man turns and **runs out the door.**

The old man looks closer at the shaggy cover. He brushes the fur aside and reads **Claws.**

A few moments later, a young woman on the street hears a man **screaming** inside the bookstore.

CHAPTER TWO

THE STOLEN BOOK

The young woman rushes inside the bookstore.

A pair of legs `stick out` from behind the counter.

The woman hears a man moaning in pain.

"Get it away from me!" says the bookseller.

The woman's eyes follow the direction that the man is pointing.

She sees a `strange book` lying on the counter.

She picks up the book.

The gold hinges **gleam**.

"This is beautiful," she says to herself.

"Help me," moans the bookseller.

The woman clutches the book to her chest, and then she hurries out the door.

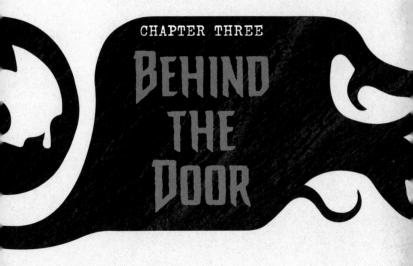

CHAPTER THREE

BEHIND THE DOOR

The young woman **rushes** into her apartment building.

The landlord sees her from his door. "You owe me rent," he calls out to her.

She hurries into her apartment and shuts the door behind her.

A few minutes later, the landlord climbs the stairs to the woman's apartment. Her rooms are dark.

The woman is missing.

The landlord sees a **dark puddle** on the floor. Next to the puddle lies a furry book.

The landlord picks up the book. "Ow!" the man yells and drops the book.

He sees the book slowly open.

The pages fold themselves into
sharp, rounded points.

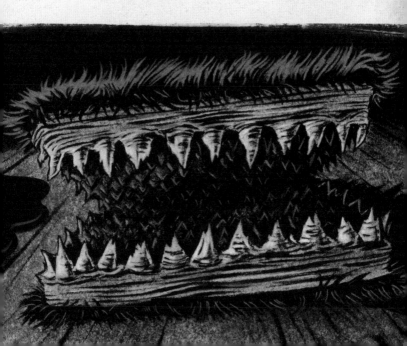

CHAPTER FOUR

THE PAPERBACK

The landlord backs away from the book on the floor. He bumps into a table. A paperback in his back pocket falls to the floor.

Ink from its pages oozes out and covers the floor.

The **puddle of ink** grows larger.

A tall, **dark shape** rises from the bubbling ink.

The ink forms into the shape of a man.

It is the Librarian.

He has been waiting inside the pages of the paperback.

He knew that the furry book would come to this apartment building, but he did not know when.

CHAPTER FIVE

THE COLLECTOR

The book leaps into the air.
Its golden hinges open as it flies
toward the Librarian's throat.

The Librarian ducks, and the
book **slams** against a wall.

With another roar, the book
flashes its teeth. It darts across the
floor and grips the Librarian's leg.

The Librarian **screams**.

The landlord is **scared**.
He runs into the hallway and
down the stairs.

Suddenly, the front door of the
building **swings** open.

A young man rushes in.

He is the same man who
sold the **strange** furry book to
the bookseller.

"Where is the book?" the young
man demands.

The landlord points up the stairs.

The Librarian has pulled the book off his leg. Blood drips onto his shoe.

He snaps his fingers. A small blue flame **bursts** from his hand.

The book backs away from the flame and crouches in a `dark corner.`

The door bangs open. It is the young man.

"That is mine," he says, pointing to the furry book.

The Librarian looks hard at the man. "The Collector," he mutters.

"Yes," says the man. "And I am here to collect my book."

"That book belongs to the Library of Doom," says the Librarian.

"It needs to be free," says the Collector. "The book is **hungry**."

"And each time the book feeds," says the Librarian, "the more **powerful** you become."

The Collector smiles. He pulls another book from his pocket and throws it through a window.

The new book hangs outside
the window and grows larger.

Quickly, the Collector jumps
onto the **floating book**.

The flying book soars away from the apartment building. It disappears into the shadowy city.

"The battle is not over yet," the Librarian says to himself.

He picks up the landlord's old paperback from the floor. The title reads *The Book that Dripped Blood.*

Then the Librarian sinks back down into the book.

Waiting.

～ THE END ～

NOTES FROM THE LIBRARIAN

Claws was once located in the Ungula Caves of the Library of Doom. Those caves are protected by steel walls ten-feet thick. They're the home for books that scratch, rip, grab, and crawl.

Claws has still not been found. The Collector has hidden it in his own private library. A library of books that he will use as an army to defeat his enemies. And I am his greatest enemy.

The Collector used to work in the Library. He was smart and hardworking. His specialty was books that screamed, sang, or whispered. Some say he was driven mad by his books. I've heard a few of the pages whisper. They still give me nightmares.

In the end, the Collector was greedy. I didn't know how greedy until the day he disappeared from the Library. He had stolen two books. One was made of diamonds. The other was made of sand.

A Page from the Library of Doom

Rare and Unusual Books

The world's bestselling book is the Bible, with almost 2.5 billion copies sold since 1815.

According to the Guinness World Records, the longest novel ever written is *In Search of Lost Time* by Marcel Proust.

The world's largest book was made by Michael Hawley of the United States in 2003. It weighs more than 130 pounds and uses enough paper to cover a football field.

Some experts say the world's smallest book is an edition of *Chameleon* by Anton Chekhov. The tiny book has thirty pages and is only a little bigger than a grain of salt.

In 1939, Frank Siebert, a medical student, raised money to buy a rare book on American Indians by selling bottles of his own blood!

About the Author

Michael Dahl is the prolific author of the bestselling *Goodnight Baseball* picture book and more than two hundred other books for children and young adults. He has won the AEP Distinguished Achievement Award three times for his nonfiction, a Teachers' Choice Award from *Learning* magazine, and a Seal of Excellence from the Creative Child Awards. Dahl currently lives in Minneapolis, Minnesota.

About the Illustrator

Bradford Kendall has enjoyed drawing for as long as he can remember. As a boy, he loved to read comic books and watch old monster movies. He graduated from the Rhode Island School of Design with a BFA in Illustration. He has owned his own commercial art business since 1983, and lives in Providence, Rhode Island, with his wife, Leigh, and their two children, Lily and Stephen. They also have a cat named Hansel and a dog named Gretel. Sometimes, they all sit together to watch an old monster movie.

Glossary

clutch (KLUTCH)—to hold tightly

mutter (MUH-tur)—to speak in a low voice with your mouth almost closed

snarl (SNARL)—to show your teeth and growl

spine (SPAHYN)—the edge of a book that holds it together

Discussion Questions

1. The first person we see with *Claws* is the
   Collector. His left arm is in a sling. What
   do you think happened to him? Is there
   any clue in the book that tells you?

2. The woman who heard the bookseller
   screaming took the book from the store.
   Why do you think she stole it? Explain
   your answer.

3. At the end of the book, the Collector
   takes *Claws* back. So why do you think
   he sold the book in the first place? What
   was his reason? Is there any clue in the
   book that tells you?

WRITING PROMPTS

1. Pretend you work at the bookstore in the first chapter. Does your store have strange books? Write a list of what they are.

2. The Collector grabs the evil book and escapes out the window. Where does he go? Write a paragraph to tell us what happens next.

3. You are walking past a bookstore when you hear a strange noise inside. What happens when you enter the store? Write your adventure!

Building the Library

Some Words from author Michael Dahl

I often make up fake titles when I'm trying to come up with ideas for books. I once made a list of titles combining books with parts of the body. Eyes? *The Book that Wore Glasses*. Feet? *The Book that Ran Away*. Blood? *The Book that Dripped* — yes! That started the idea that eventually turned into this book.

Like the heroic Librarian, all of my villains are connected with books — the Collector, the Eraser, the Spellbinder, Atlas. I'd like to create a bad guy who folds paper into weapons. The Origami Master? Origami Mummy? Or maybe one who traps people inside coffin-sized books. Buried Beneath the Covers? Book Ends? Luckily, there are as many adventures in the Library of Doom as there are books on its shelves!

EXPLORE THE ENTIRE
LIBRARY OF DOOM

THE SMASHING SCROLL
BY MICHAEL DAHL

THE BOOK THAT DRIPPED BLOOD
BY MICHAEL DAHL

POISON PAGES

THE BEAST BENEATH THE STAIRS

ATTACK OF THE PAPER BATS
BY MICHAEL DAHL

THE EYE IN THE GRAVEYARD
BY MICHAEL DAHL

THE DIGITAL ARCHIVES